LA Vamp

Book 1

Angela Lartey

LA Vamp by Angela Lartey

ISBN 978-1-952027-50-5 (Paperback)
ISBN 978-1-952027-51-2 (Hardback)
ISBN 978-1-952027-52-9 (eBook)

This book is written to provide information and motivation to readers. Its purpose is not to render any type of psychological, legal, or professional advice of any kind. The content is the sole opinion and expression of the author, and not necessarily that of the publisher.

Printed in the United States of America.

New Leaf Media, LLC
175 S. 3rd Street, Suite 200
Columbus, OH 43215
www.thenewleafmedia.com

Act 1

Chas: Why are you not smiling?

Annabel: Because I am upset.

Chas: Upset about what?

Annabel: The cheerleading team.

Chas: What about it?

Annabel: The girls don't seem to like me.

Chas: Don't be silly. Of course they like you.

Annabel: No, they don't. You see, Chas, I am a book-loving girl.

At an opposite table.

Ash: If only I could befriend Annabel.

Toby, *to James*: Who are you texting?

James: My father in Japan.

Ash: What's he doing there?

James: Working.

Toby: Boy, your dad sure likes to travel.

Ash: What do you expect from a businessman?

James: He's a movie producer.

Chas's voice: What do you mean you are quitting the cheerleading team?

Annabel's voice: It's just not me.

Chas's voice: It *is* for you. You're pretty and slim.

Annabel's voice: Goodbye, Chas.

Chas's voice: Hey, come back here this instant. Don't make me chase after you!

James: Sounds to me like Annabel's boyfriend has been burned.

Toby: Gives her a chance to be friends with people her own age.

Ash: Well, if it's true that she and that control freak of a boyfriend are done, then I am in.

Toby:	I am going to get a toffee yogurt. You guys want anything?
James:	A chocolate-flavoured frozen yogurt.
Ash:	A strawberry jelly with cream.

Toby goes to the dessert counter.

James:	The weekend is just around the corner.
Ash:	Yep.
James:	I am so glad.

Toby returns.

Toby:	They did not have chocolate, so I got you butterscotch.
James:	That's OK.
Toby:	So what are you guys talking about?
Ash:	The weekend.

Chas's voice:	Quit making a scene.
Annabel's voice:	Stay away from me!
Chas's voice:	So that's it? You're going to leave your master?
Annabel's voice:	You don't own me, Chas!
Chas's voice:	You signed a contract to be with me until death do you part.
Annabel's voice:	You forced me to sign it.
Chas's voice:	This is not the time or place for you to have a psychotic breakdown.
Annabel's voice:	Psychotic breakdown? Don't make me laugh. You're a dog, Chas.
Chas's voice:	Do you mind keeping your voice down?
Annabel's voice:	It's over, Chas.

Toby:	Sounds like Annabel has broken her silence.

Ash takes out his phone.

James:	What are you doing, Ash?
Ash:	Texting my auntie the good news.
James:	Why?
Ash:	So she does not have to come to the school.
James:	To do what?
Ash:	To talk to the school counsellor about my concerns about Annabel and Chas.
James:	Can't you just tell her the news when you return home?
Toby:	Put your phone away. Chas is heading this way. Pretend we don't know what just happened.
Chas, on his phone:	*She's lost it. My blonde beauty just walked away without any explanation.*

The boys take their trays and put their rubbish in the bins. They add their trays to a pile and leave the canteen.

Toby:	What is the plan?
Ash:	To find Annabel.

They see a group of cheerleaders huddled in a corner.

Cheerleader 2:	Thank God she quit the team.
Cheerleader 1:	I never liked her in the first place.
Cheerleader 3:	Now Chas is free. I can slowly move in.
Cheerleader 4:	And do what?
Cheerleader 3:	Well, everything.

Cheerleader 2:	Like what?
Cheerleader 3:	Talking, flirting, give him my number, and show him my D cups.
Cheerleader 1:	Really!

The boys walk past them.

James:	Well, those cheerleaders seem happy.
Ash:	So Annabel must be nearby.

The girl's bathroom door opens, and Annabel walks out.

Ash:	Bingo.
James:	How are you doing, Annabel?
Annabel:	Hi, James.
Toby:	How is everything?
Annabel:	Good, I guess.
Ash:	Is everything OK with Chas?
Annabel:	The fool called me psychotic.
Ash:	That's mean of him.
Annabel:	The main reason I went out with him was to prevent him from sending indecent images of me to his friends on Instagram.
James:	What were you thinking?
Annabel:	I was stupidly in love.
Toby:	When did this all start?
Annabel	The day I started here.
James:	Doing anything this coming weekend?
Annabel:	Beside my grandparents coming to stay, nothing.
Ash:	Let's go to the mall.
Annabel:	All right.

Ash:	And then the ice cream parlour and then the beach.
Annabel:	Sounds great! What time should I be at the mall?
Ash:	My auntie will pick you up.
Annabel:	I don't feel comfortable being picked up.
Ash:	Don't worry. My auntie will not bite.
Annabel:	Well, if you say so.
Ash:	I and the boys will be at your house at around 11.35 a.m.
Annabel:	Sounds OK to me.
James:	See you in class.

Annabel smiles as Ash and his friends walk away.

Toby:	Well, that was easy.
Ash:	We are not out of the woods yet.
James:	What do you mean?
Ash:	We have to treat her like a princess.
Toby:	There is no way we are going to spoil her.
Ash:	I mean by guarding her.
Toby:	Oh, OK.

They go outside.

Act 2

Tony:	What would you like?
Nancie:	A chicken burger with large fries and a large strawberry milkshake.
Tony:	I will have the same, but with a mango milkshake.
Nancie:	Mango milkshake? Is that new?
Tony:	It's been advertised since June.
Nancie:	Oh.

Angry man's voice   Where is my Triple-X burger, supersize fries, and drink?

Woman's voice: Sir, do you mind keeping your voice down?

Angry man's voice: I want my Triple-X burger, supersize fries, and drink!

Woman's voice: Sir, I am asking you again to keep your voice down.

Angry man's voice: I paid fourteen dollars for my meal. Where is it?

Nancie:	How is everyone?
Tony:	They're fine.
Nancie:	Is your baby cousin talking?
Tony:	She's getting there. She learned a new word today.
Nancie:	What was the new word?
Tony:	"Poopy" Grandpa.
Nancie:	That's not a very nice word.
Tony:	That's because she saw him taking a dump in the toilet.

Angry man's voice: I am giving you the count of three to give me my food, or I will walk out of here.

Nancie:	Have your auntie and uncle thought of putting your cousin in day care?
Tony:	They're still deciding whether to go private or public.
Nancie:	Are your auntie and uncle willing to pay for private day care?
Tony:	If they can pay for my private education, they can do the same for my cousin.

Woman's voice:	Here is you order, sir.
Angry man's voice:	Thank you!
Woman's voice:	Have a nice day. Next, please.
Tony:	One chicken burger with large fries and a strawberry milkshake. And the same thing but with a mango milkshake.

Woman:	Sorry, we are out of mango.

Tony:	OK, then banana.
Woman:	That will be $12.50.

Tony pays the woman.

Woman:	Here is your change.
Tony:	Thank you.
Nancie:	Doing anything tonight?
Tony:	Just playing with my cousin and making sure my brother does not stay up too late.
Nancie:	OK.
Tony:	Why do you ask?
Nancie:	No reason.
Tony:	Were you planning something?
Nancie:	Oh, no.

Woman:	Here is your order, sir.
Tony:	Thank you.
Woman:	Have a nice day.

Tony and Nancie take their food and walk away.

Nancie:	Such a nice day.
Tony:	Yeah.
Nancie:	Do you like living in Los Angeles?
Tony:	Yes, I do.
Nancie:	What about your auntie and uncle?
Tony:	They like it here too.
Nancie:	So, tell me about your vampire status.
Tony:	There's not much to say besides having a seven-incher.
Nancie:	You have a seven-incher?
Tony:	Of course.
Nancie:	Sounds naughty.
Tony:	You will see it sooner or later.
Nancie:	I would love that.
Tony:	I knew you were going to say that.

Nancie and Tony kiss.

Tony:	So you like a big manhood.
Nancie:	The bigger, the better.
Tony:	Where do you want me to put it?
Nancie:	In my fat vagina.
Tony:	Come on. You are not that fat.
Nancie:	I applied for a job and was rejected.
Tony:	What job did you apply for?

Nancie:	An air hostess.
Tony:	For which airline?
Nancie:	No comment.
Tony:	OK.
Nancie:	It's like everywhere you go, you have to be model perfect.
Tony:	You don't have to look and envy other people's bodies.
Nancie:	It's not that I envy slim people, because my sister is slim. It's the fact that it is constantly in people's faces.
Tony:	Well, I like you just the way you are.

Nancie smiles.

Tony:	You will find another job.
Nancie:	Where?
Tony:	There are many jobs you can apply for.
Nancie:	Like what?
Tony:	That's for you to find out.

Act 3

Doncaster:	Honey, have you see my … Geez, Father, what the hell?
Doncaster's father:	Can't an old vampire sit naked while reading the newspaper?
Doncaster:	No!

Monica and Narnia walk into the living room.

Monica:	I have made a final decision about Narnia's day care.
Doncaster:	You have?
Monica:	Why is your father naked?
Doncaster:	Because he's old and senile.
Doncaster's father:	So which one are you applying for?
Monica:	Well, because of Narnia's speech development, I say private.
Doncaster:	I don't think the teachers at a private day care will appreciate the word *poop*.
Doncaster's father:	Oh, bleh, bleh!
Doncaster:	And besides, I don't have twelve hundred dollars to pay every term.
Monica:	You did it for Ash.
Doncaster:	That's because he is gifted.
Monica:	So is your daughter.
Doncaster:	Dear, I know you want the best for our little girl.
Monica:	There is no way I am putting Narnia in public day care.

Monica and Narnia leave.

Doncaster's father:	Someone is not going to get sex tonight.
Doncaster:	Shut up, and put on some clothes.

Doncaster's father: Go and see to your girlfriend.

Doncaster leaves.

Doncaster's father: Finally, I can read the newspaper in peace.

Monica reads to Narnia in the master bedroom.

Monica: So the three bears went for a walk when along came Goldilocks.

Doncaster: Reading *Goldilocks and the Three Bears*?

Monica: When did you come in?

Doncaster: Still angry with me?

Monica: What do you think?

Doncaster: Could you put Narnia in her bedroom for a second?

Monica picks up Narnia and carries her out from the master bedroom. Narnia starts to cry.

Monica: It's only for a second. Mummy will come back.

She closes the door. Monica turns and walks back over to the master bedroom.

Doncaster: Sit down on the bed.

Monica: OK.

Monica sits on the bed.

Doncaster: It's not that I do not want Narnia to have the best education.

Monica:	She's a smart girl. Tell me what one-and-a-half-year-old can say Daddy, Mummy, and Grandpa in full?
Doncaster:	I think most one-and-a-half-year-olds can say those words in full.
Monica:	I just want our daughter to go into private education.
Doncaster:	All right, I will see what I can do.
Monica:	I have a prospectus of the day care I want our daughter to attend.
Doncaster:	You do?
Monica:	It was given to me by a mother over at the mother and baby centre.
Doncaster:	OK.
Monica:	Do you want to see?
Doncaster:	Please.

Monica picks up a prospectus from the bedside table and gives it to Doncaster.

Doncaster:	Let's see what my father thinks.
Doncaster's father:	See what?
Doncaster:	How long have you been standing there?
Doncaster's father:	Long enough to give you this prospectus.

Doncaster's father walks over to Monica and Doncaster.

Doncaster's father:	It's a daycare that is attached to an elementary school.
Doncaster:	Really?
Doncaster's father:	I went to look at it, and the results were perfect.
Monica:	But I want my daughter to go into private education.

Doncaster:	Maybe we should all go downstairs for some tea.
Monica:	I want something much better than just tea.
Doncaster:	Lemonade?
Monica:	Perfect.

Doncaster turns and walks out from the master bedroom, heading to Narnia's bedroom. He opens the door to see her fast asleep in her cot. He quietly closes the door and walks back into the master bedroom.

Monica:	How is she?
Doncaster:	Fast asleep in her cot.
Doncaster's father:	We must consider getting her a bed.
Doncaster:	Wait until she is two.

Monica, Doncaster, and his father walk out from the master bedroom. They walk along the corridor over to the stairs. As they go down, Doncaster's phone rings in his trouser pocket. He takes it out.

Doncaster:	Hello?
Tony's voice:	*Hello, Uncle, it's me. I am just calling to say I am with Nancie and heading to the beach.*
Doncaster:	That's fine. Remember to pick up your brother from school later.
Tony's voice:	*I will, Uncle.*
Doncaster:	OK, goodbye.

Doncaster puts his phone in his trouser pocket.

Act 4

Tony:	To the beach we go.
Nancie:	Where all the hot men and women hang out.
Tony:	You're still body envious?
Nancie:	What if these hot skinny women start calling me names and give me the look?
Tony:	What look?
Nancie:	Of disgust.
Tony:	If they do, then there are shallow and need to get a life.
Nancie:	It will be like high school again.
Tony:	What happened in high school?
Nancie:	Everything from gum being put in my hair to name-calling and abuse.
Tony:	Abuse?
Nancie:	Not physical abuse, but *Family Guy* abuse.
Tony:	Oh!
Nancie:	My sister was different. High school boys will try to get into her panties; and popular girls will try to get into fights with her just because she is pretty.
Tony:	What kind of a high school did you and your sister attend?
Nancie:	Some high school in North Beverly Hills. And you?
Tony:	A comprehensive private school for boys.
Nancie:	Were you bullied?
Tony:	Not really.
Nancie:	Oh. I was thinking you were because you're a vampire.
Tony:	Actually, I was treated like any other boy in that school.
Nancie:	You were?
Tony:	Yes. No one knew that I was different.
Nancie:	What about the teachers?
Tony:	Not even the teachers.
Nancie:	OK.

Tony:	How about we find a private spot on the beach so we can study each other's roger zones?
Nancie:	Not until you treat me to an ice cream.

Tony's car turns into the beach car park. A group of boys looks at them as Tony parks the car.

Nancie:	I don't like the look those boys are giving us.
Tony:	Just calm down.

Nancie opens the car door and steps out.

Boy 1 yells:	Do you have a warrant for that big ass of yours?
Boy 2 yells:	What are you, African American?
Nancie to self:	*Just ignore them, and you will be okay.*
Boy 3 yells:	Twerk that booty, bitch!

Tony steps out from the car.

Tony:	All right.
Nancie:	Yeah.

They both close the car door

Boy 1 yells:	Bro, what's with the tattoo on your neck?
Boy 2 yells:	Is it some kind of a code?

Nancie and Tony walk away from the car and go to the stairs. They go down.

Nancie:	So did you take part in any school activity?

Tony:	Not really.
Nancie:	Me neither.

Tony and Nancie go on the beach. The two of them kiss.

Tony:	Now, let's get you that ice cream.
Nancie:	All right.

A beer can hit the side of Nancie's face.

Voice:	*Fat-ass bitch!*
Nancie:	Let's get out from this place.

Tony and Nancie start walking along the beach.

Tony:	Is your sister OK?
Nancie:	Yes, she is fine.

They come to an ice cream stand.

Ice cream woman:	Well, aren't you a nice couple.
Tony:	Thank you.
Ice cream woman:	What can I get you both?
Tony:	One vanilla ice cream.
Nancie:	And a rocky road for me.
Ice cream woman:	Coming right up. So how long have you been together?
Nancie:	Since March.
Ice cream woman:	That's so sweet. Here are your ice creams.
Nancie:	Thanks.

Tony pays the ice cream woman.

Ice cream woman: Thanks. Enjoy your day.

Tony and Nancie turn and walk away.

Tony: Now to find a spot to get studying.
Nancie: How about over there?
Tony: It looks occupied. How about over there by those empty stands?
Nancie: Sounds perfect.

The two of them walk over to the stands and sit down.

Tony: Ready?
Nancie: I have something to say before we get studying. I'm kind of sensitive down below, just to let you know.
Tony: I will be gentle.

Tony and Nancie start kissing.

Nancie: Are you nervous?
Tony: Not at all.

Tony unbuttons Nancie's shorts. The two of them start kissing as he slowly pulls them down.

Tony: You like that?
Nancie: We have not even started.

The two of them carry on kissing.

Nancie: I almost forgot. Are you carrying protection?

Act 5

Cheerleader 3:	What are you doing after school?
Chas:	Just hanging out with friends over at the park.
Cheerleader 3:	I and the other cheerleaders heard that you and Annabel broke up.
Chas:	Yes.
Cheerleader 3:	Why's that?
Chas:	It just wasn't working out between the two of us.
Cheerleader 3:	Oh. Never mind. You will find another.
Chas:	It's not all the time I come across a girl like Annabel.
Cheerleader 3:	Well, she's gone. Time to move on.
Chas:	Hay, Caroline.
Cheerleader 3:	Yes, Chas?
Chas:	Can you do me a favour?
Cheerleader 3:	Sure.
Chas:	Do you have Instagram or Snapchat?
Cheerleader 3:	Yes, why?
Chas:	I am going to send you some pics of my ex.
Cheerleader 3:	Okay.
Chas:	I want the whole school to know the type of girl my ex is.
Cheerleader 3:	All right, hit me with them.
Chas:	All right, here are the first few.
Cheerleader 3:	Dang. Are you sure you want me to send these kinds of pics throughout the whole school?
Chas:	Don't worry—she's my ex.
Cheerleader 3:	But it's child pornography.
Chas:	Do you want to be more popular?
Cheerleader 3:	Well, yeah!
Chas:	Then do as you are told.

Chas walks away. The other cheerleaders walk over to Caroline.

Cheerleader 4:   Well.
Cheerleader 3:   Well, what?
Cheerleader 1:   Did you and Chas hook up?
Cheerleader 3:   Kind of.
Cheerleader 2:   Oh, good!
Cheerleader 4:   We should celebrate.
Cheerleader 3:   Not just yet. I have to do something before we can go out.
Cheerleader 1:   OK.
Cheerleader 2:   What do you have to do?
Cheerleader 3:   I have to send pics of his ex throughout the school.
Cheerleader 1:   What kind of pics?
Cheerleader 3:   These.

The cheerleaders laugh.

Cheerleader 3:   It's no laughing matter!
Cheerleader 2:   Talk about a pre-teen slut.
Cheerleader 1:   Are those her boobies or an allergic reaction?
Cheerleader 4:   Has she ever heard of waxing?
Cheerleader 3:   Stop it. This is serious.
Cheerleader 2:   Oh, come on, Caroline. You hate the girl.
Cheerleader 3:   Yeah, but this is a step too far.
Cheerleader 1:   What step too far?
Cheerleader 4:   You always considered this girl a tramp.
Cheerleader 3:   Yeah.
Cheerleader 2:   Well, this is your chance.
Cheerleader 1:   To show her true colours.
Cheerleader 3:   I could be expelled and put in jail.

Cheerleader 4:	Make it anonymous.
Cheerleader 2:	That way nobody will know who sent them.
Cheerleader 1:	Or you can send them and then delete the evidence from your phone.
Cheerleader 2:	It's your choice.
Cheerleader 3:	All right, I will send and delete the pics from my phone.
Cheerleader 4:	Good choice.
Cheerleader 1:	Now, let's get the ball rolling.
Cheerleader 3:	All right.

Act 6

Monica on the telephone:	Hello, is this the Teddy Bear Day Care Centre?
Woman's voice:	Yes, how can I help you?
Monica:	I am calling to find out if you have any spaces at your day care centre.
Doncaster:	There is no way I am massaging your feet.
Doncaster's father:	Why?
Doncaster:	Because every time I massage your feet, you laugh and pass wind.
Doncaster's father:	I don't crack wind when you massage my feet.
Doncaster:	Yes, you do.
Doncaster's father:	Just massage my feet!

Doncaster begins massaging his father's feet.

Doncaster's father:	So nice of you to massage my feet.
Monica:	*Narnia.*
Woman's voice:	*How old is she?*
Monica:	*She's almost two.*
Woman's voice:	*Almost two? OK, I am afraid we don't have any spaces at the moment.*
Monica:	*OK.*
Woman's voice:	*But I will let you know in the future if there are any spaces available.*
Monica:	*OK. It was nice talking to you. Goodbye.*

Monica puts down the telephone.

Doncaster:	Does Narnia have a place in day care?
Monica:	No.
Doncaster's father:	No?

Monica:	The lady said she will let me know in the future if there are any spaces available.
Doncaster's father:	There is no way I am paying for private day care.
Monica:	Well, at this rate, you may have to go private if we cannot get Narnia a placed in public day care.
Doncaster's father:	Try another number.
Monica:	Okay.

Narnia walks into the living room. She goes over to Doncaster.

Doncaster:	Hello, sweetie. Did you have a nice nap?

Narnia picks up a pink teddy bear. She gives it to Doncaster's father.

Doncaster's father:	Is that teddy bear for me?
Monica on the telephone:	Hello, is this Mother Goose Day Care Centre?
Man's voice:	Yes, it is. How can I help you, miss?
Monica:	Do you by any chance have spaces at your daycare?
Man's voice:	Indeed I have. May I ask from where you are calling?
Monica:	Beverley Hills East.
Man's voice:	OK, may I ask what is your name?
Monica:	Miss Magee.
Man's voice:	OK, and your child's name?
Monica:	Narnia.
Man's voice:	How old is she?
Monica:	She's almost two.

Man's voice:	Almost two? OK. Is she going to be full-time or part-time?
Monica:	There are two times?
Man's voice:	Yes.
Monica:	Hold on. Let me ask my partner and his father.
Doncaster:	What is it, darling?
Monica:	Is Narnia going to be at day care full-time or part-time?
Doncaster's father:	Who's asking?
Monica:	A man on the telephone.
Doncaster:	A man on the telephone?
Doncaster's father:	Pass the telephone to me.

Monica gives the telephone to Doncaster's father.

Doncaster's father:	Hello?
Man's voice:	Hello, are you the man of the house?
Doncaster's father:	No, I am the father to the man of the house.
Man's voice:	OK, I just want to know if your granddaughter is going to be in day care full-time or part-time.
Doncaster's father:	Just before I go any further, may I ask your name?
Man's voice:	It's Donovan. I am the teacher at Mother Goose Day Care.
Doncaster's father:	OK, where are you based?
Man's voice:	Bel Air.
Doncaster's father:	OK, and do you have spaces available?
Man's voice:	Yes.
Doncaster's father:	All right, and you want to know if my granddaughter is going to do part-time or full-time?
Man's voice:	Yes.
Narnia:	Poop-poop!
Doncaster:	You want to go poop-poop? Go to Mummy.

Monica picks up Narnia and walks out from the living room.

Doncaster's father:	Her speech is really good, so I suggest full-time.
Man's voice:	All right, no problem. Does your granddaughter have any allergic reactions?
Doncaster's father:	Not that I know of.
Man's voice:	Medical conditions?
Doncaster's father:	No.
Man's voice:	No problem. Do you know your way round?
Doncaster's father:	Very well, yes.
Man's voice:	Good. Let me just give you the details about where we are at.
Doncaster's father:	OK, wonderful.

Monica comes back into the living room.

Doncaster:	She's going to be in day care full-time.
Monica:	OK. I may have to do some shopping.
Doncaster:	Just a backpack will do. A nice little Hello Kitty backpack.
Monica:	I was thinking more Disney princess.
Doncaster:	Oh, OK.
Doncaster's father:	*Thanks for the location. I will tell them. Goodbye.*

Doncaster's father puts down the telephone.

Doncaster's father:	She starts next Monday.
Monica:	Wonderful.

Monica's phone rings in her skirt pocket. She takes it out.

Monica:	Hello?
Tony's voice:	I am in a crisis.
Monica:	What happened?
Tony's voice:	I do not have any baby-preventing balloons.
Monica:	What are you doing, having a moment of passion?
Tony's voice:	Two reasons. One, I promised her. And two, I am horny.
Monica:	Well, be un-horny and think of making your way to Ash's school.
Tony's voice:	It's that time already?
Monica:	Yes.
Tony's voice:	All right.

Monica puts her phone back in her skirt pocket.

Doncaster:	Was that Tony?
Monica:	Yes.
Doncaster's father:	What does he want?
Monica:	Condoms.
Doncaster's father:	OK, why does he want condoms?

Narnia walks into the living room.

Narnia:	Tea party.
Doncaster:	You want to play with your tea party set?

Narnia walks over to a white and pink table with chairs at the corner of the living room. She begins playing.

Act 7

Tony and Nancie in the car.

Nancie:	How can you not have protection?
Tony:	I did not realise.
Nancie:	Anyway, I really enjoyed our time together at the beach.
Tony:	Beside the fact we did not do anything?
Nancie:	Don't worry. I am not that fussed about losing my virginity at the early stages of our relationship.
Tony:	You're not?
Nancie:	No.
Tony:	Me neither.
Nancie:	So where are we heading to?
Tony:	To pick up my brother from school.
Nancie:	How old is he?
Tony:	He's thirteen.
Nancie:	I remember when I was thirteen. Full of acne, hair in side plaits with white thickly framed glasses.
Tony:	I did not know you wore glasses.
Nancie:	I did. I looked like a blonde Meg from *Family Guy*.
Tony:	And now you look like a Disney princess.
Nancie:	Which one?
Tony:	Sleeping Beauty.
Nancie:	Thanks. Better than Roly-Poly or fat-ass Annie.
Tony:	Were those the names you were called in high school?
Nancie:	Yes, and many more.
Tony:	Let's talk more about your sister.
Nancie:	OK.
Tony:	Is she older than you?
Nancie:	We are twins.
Tony:	Twins?

Nancie:	But we are not identical.
Tony:	Not identical?
Nancie:	She was born two minutes before me.
Tony:	Really?
Nancie:	Yes.
Tony:	Does she go to work?
Nancie:	She's at college.
Tony:	Studying what?
Nancie:	Psychology.
Tony:	Psychology?
Nancie:	She wants to help people.
Tony:	That's cool.

The car stops at the lights. A group of young men in a yellow sports car looks at them.

Nancie:	I do not like the way those young men are looking at us.
Tony:	Relax.

The lights turn green. The car drives away. The yellow sports car follows.

Nancie:	They are following us.
Tony:	Don't panic.

The yellow sports car turns and drives away.

Nancie:	OK.
Tony:	There wasn't any need to panic.

*The car arrives at a school parking lot. Ash, his two friends,
and a girl are standing outside the school's entrance.*

Toby: You are in safe hands.

James: Forget all about what has happened in school today.

Annabel: My life is over.

Ash: Just relax, and don't feel sorry about yourself.

Annabel: I will try.

Ash: Good. I will see you tomorrow.

Annabel, Toby, and James turn and walk away.

Tony: Have a good day at school?

Car door opens.

Ash: There is a rumour that this girl's photos have gone
                   viral.

Tony: OK.

*Ash climbs into the back of the car. He closes the door. The
car drives out from the school parking lot.*

Ash: Who's this?

Tony: This is Nancie, my girlfriend.

Ash: Your girlfriend?

Tony: Yes.

Ash: She is kind of chubby.

Tony: Do you want to walk home?

Ash: I mean chubby in a good way.

Tony: There is no such thing as chubby in a good way.

Nancie:	It's all right. Tony.
Ash:	So tell me. Nancie. How long have you been dating my brother?
Nancie:	Since March.
Ash:	How did you meet?
Nancie:	At the mall.
Ash:	What was your response when you saw my brother?
Nancie:	Thanks for protecting me.
Ash:	What kind of response is that?
Tony:	She was being followed.
Ash:	By whom?
Nancie:	A dirty old man was following me around.
Ash:	Oh.
Tony:	So tell me about this girl.
Ash:	Her name is Annabel. She is in my class. She just broke up with her boyfriend, and now she is in hot water.
Tony:	OK.
Nancie:	May I ask how old was this girl's boyfriend?
Ash:	Fifteen.
Nancie:	And how old is this girl in your class?
Ash:	Thirteen.
Tony:	What's a thirteen-year-old doing going out with a fifteen-year-old?

Act 8

Ash:	I don't know.
Tony:	So what did you learn today?
Ash:	Biology, math, Latin, and French.
Tony:	OK, cool.
Nancie:	I remember doing those subjects in high school.
Ash:	Do you how long ago was that?
Nancie:	Let's see. I am twenty now, so around two years ago.
Ash:	Really?
Nancie:	Yes.
Ash:	Hey, Tony, can we stop at the ice cream parlour?
Tony:	No.
Ash:	Why?
Tony:	You are going to eat dinner when you get home.

The car stops at the lights.

Ash:	Please?
Tony:	No.
Ash:	Don't make me tell your girlfriend about your stash of adult manga comic books.
Nancie:	You re into Manga?
Tony:	What are you doing, snooping in my bedroom!
Ash:	You should really find a good place to hide them.
Nancie:	Soft-core or hardcore?
Tony:	Can we just change the subject?
Ash:	Hot lesbians and oral action.
Nancie: Really?	
Tony:	Enough!

The lights turn green. Tony drives.

Ash:	I have to hide my face in shame and embarrassment every time we go to that section at Comic Con.
Tony:	I said enough!
Ash:	Can we?
Tony:	Can we what?
Ash:	Stop over at the ice cream parlour?
Tony:	No.
Ash:	Then I shall carry on.

The car turns into the ice cream parlour parking lot. The car stops. Ash opens the door and climbs out. He closes the door and goes in.

Nancie:	You did not have to do that.
Tony:	Anything to stop him from talking.
Nancie:	What is your aunt's name?
Tony:	Monica.
Nancie:	And your uncle's name?
Tony:	Doncaster.
Nancie:	And your grandfather?
Tony:	Nixon.

Ash opens the car door. He climbs in and closes the door.

Ash:	Nothing like a toffee and coffee ice cream sundae.
Tony:	Did you say coffee?
Ash:	Yes.
Tony:	What did Uncle say about getting things with caffeine?
Ash:	Eh.
Tony:	Go and change it.

Silent.

Tony: I said go and change that ice cream!

Silent.

Tony: Fine, all right, but don't come into my bedroom complaining about being reckless and having a lack of sleep.

The car drives away from the ice cream parlour parking lot.

Annabel: I regret sending my ex those photos.
James: Don't worry about it.
Annabel: What if it goes viral for paedophiles to see and get excited?
Toby: No paedophile is going to see it.
Annabel: The worst thing is my parents seeing their angelic daughter's nude pics on their phones and desktop.

A red car with dark windows pulls up beside them. The window comes down.

Woman's voice: Would you like to try some weed?
Toby: No, thank you.
James: I don't want to end up like my brother and his partner.
Annabel: I will.
Toby: No!
Annabel: I don't see the point of life anymore.
James: So turning to a drug junkie is going to help with the situation?

Toby:	Do you want to be a lady scientist and find the course for cancer and other illnesses?
Annabel:	Yes.
James:	Well, don't go down that path.

The red car drives away.

Toby:	I did not know your brother was a weed addict.
James:	There are lots of things you don't know about my family.

Toby's phone rings in his school bag. He opens it and takes it out.

Toby:	Hello?
Toby's dad's voice:	Can you stop by the police station?
Toby:	Yeah, all right. Would you like me to pick up some Krispy Kreme on the way?
Toby's dad's voice:	No.
Toby:	What about coffee?
Toby's dad's voice:	No Krispy Kreme or coffee. Just come to the police station so that I can give you a ride home.
Toby:	Yes, Dad.
Toby's dad's voice:	Good.

Toby puts his phone back in his school bag.

Toby:	Sorry, guys. I must go.
James:	OK, see you tomorrow.

Toby crosses the road.

James:	Well, it's just us now.
Annabel:	Yes.

A white BMW stops beside them. The door opens. A tall man with blond hair wearing a white suit comes out of the car.

Man:	Are you Annabel Wilson?
Annabel:	Yes.
Man:	I am Jeffry, one of your father's work colleague. Would you like a ride home?
Annabel:	Only if my friend comes along. I am a little sensitive right now.
Man:	Fine, just come in the car.

James and Annabel walk over to the car. They open the door and climb in. The door shuts, and the car drives away.

Man:	Did you have a nice day at school?
Annabel:	Not really.
James:	She is a target of a rumour.
Man:	What rumour is that?
Annabel:	I don't wish to comment.
Man:	Well, whatever it is, tell your parents.
Annabel:	That's if I have the courage to do so.
Man:	What do you mean?
Annabel:	It is personal.
Man:	How personal?
Annabel:	Very.
Man:	Can't I at least get a bit of info?
James:	She said personal!
Tony:	Bel Air, you say?

Ash:	What happened to the day care centres here in East Beverly Hills?
Doncaster:	Full up.
Tony:	How can all the day care centres here be full up?
Doncaster's father:	A lot more children have been born ever since you and Ash were Narnia's age.
Ash:	So is granddad going to pay?
Doncaster:	It's a public day care.
Ash:	A public day care in Bel Air.
Tony:	Does she have to wear a uniform?
Doncaster's father:	I don't think so.
Tony:	I don't like my cousin mixing with rich kids.
Ash:	It will spoil her self-esteem.
Tony:	The least thing I want is my cousin asking for a pony.
Ash:	Or wanting to enter into beauty pageants.
Doncaster:	So what do you want granddad to do? Call to say that we have changed our minds?
Ash and Tony:	Yes.
Doncaster's father:	Not going to happen.

Monica and Narnia walk into the living room.

Monica on phone:	*I don't know anyone of that name.*
Doncaster:	Whom are you talking to, dear?
Monica:	My mother.
Doncaster:	What's happened?
Monica:	My brother has come back.

www.ingramcontent.com/pod-product-compliance
Lightning Source LLC
Chambersburg PA
CBHW071842190726
48292CB00005B/1880